The Adventures of Harold and the Purple Crayon

Four Magical Stories

Written and illustrated by

Crockett Johnson

CONTENTS

HARPERCOLLINSPUBLISHERS

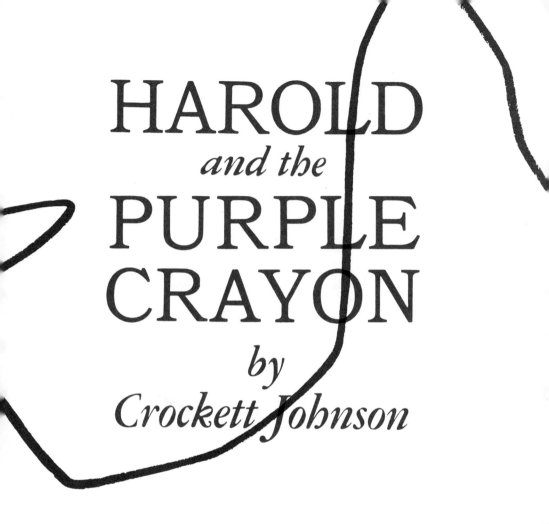

HAROLD
and the
PURPLE CRAYON

by
Crockett Johnson

 HarperCollins*Publishers*

Copyright © 1955 by Crockett Johnson
Copyright renewed 1983 by Ruth Krauss
All rights reserved. Printed in the U.S.A.
Library of Congress catalog card number: 55–7683
ISBN: 0–06–022935–7
ISBN: 0–06–022936–5 (lib. bdg.)
ISBN: 0–06–443022–7 (pbk.)

One evening, after thinking it over for
some time, Harold decided to go for a walk
in the moonlight.

There wasn't any moon, and Harold needed a
moon for a walk in the moonlight.

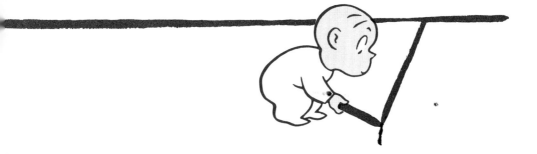

And he needed something to walk on.

He made a long straight path so he wouldn't
get lost.

And he set off on his walk, taking his big
purple crayon with him.

But he didn't seem to be getting anywhere
on the long straight path.

So he left the path for a short cut across
a field. And the moon went with him.

The short cut led right to where Harold thought a forest ought to be.

He didn't want to get lost in the woods.
So he made a very small forest, with just
one tree in it.

It turned out to be an apple tree.

The apples would be very tasty, Harold
thought, when they got red.

So he put a frightening dragon under the tree to guard the apples.

It was a terribly frightening dragon.

It even frightened Harold. He backed away.

His hand holding the purple crayon shook.

Suddenly he realized what was happening.

But by then Harold was over his head in
an ocean.

He came up thinking fast.

And in no time he was climbing aboard a trim little boat.

He quickly set sail.

And the moon sailed along with him.

After he had sailed long enough, Harold
made land without much trouble.

He stepped ashore on the beach, wondering
where he was.

The sandy beach reminded Harold of picnics.

And the thought of picnics made him hungry.

So he laid out a nice simple picnic lunch.

There was nothing but pie.

But there were all nine kinds of pie that
Harold liked best.

When Harold finished his picnic there was
quite a lot left.

He hated to see so much delicious pie go
to waste.

So Harold left a very hungry moose and a
deserving porcupine to finish it up.

And, off he went, looking for a hill to
climb, to see where he was.

Harold knew that the higher up he went,
the farther he could see. So he decided
to make the hill into a mountain.

If he went high enough, he thought, he
could see the window of his bedroom.

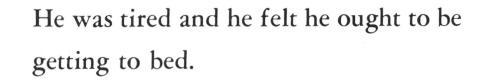

He was tired and he felt he ought to be getting to bed.

He hoped he could see his bedroom window
from the top of the mountain.

But as he looked down over the other side

he slipped—

And there wasn't any other side of the
mountain. He was falling, in thin air.

But, luckily, he kept his wits and his
purple crayon.

He made a balloon and he grabbed on to it.

And he made a basket under the balloon big
enough to stand in.

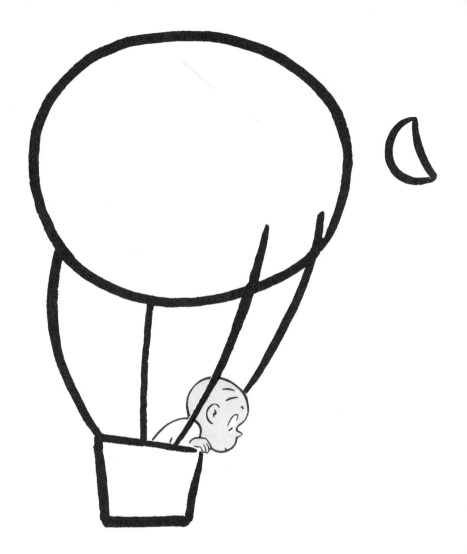

He had a fine view from the balloon but he
couldn't see his window. He couldn't even
see a house.

So he made a house, with windows.

And he landed the balloon on the grass in
the front yard.

None of the windows was his window.

He tried to think where his window ought
to be.

He made some more windows.

He made a big building full of windows.

He made lots of buildings full of windows.

He made a whole city full of windows.

But none of the windows was his window.

He couldn't think where it might be.

He decided to ask a policeman.

The policeman pointed the way Harold was
going anyway. But Harold thanked him.

And he walked along with the moon,
wishing he was in his room and in bed.

Then, suddenly, Harold remembered.

He remembered where his bedroom window
was, when there was a moon.

It was always right around the moon.

And then Harold made his bed.

He got in it and he drew up the covers.

The purple crayon dropped on the floor.
And Harold dropped off to sleep.

Harold's Fairy Tale

to the
enchanted
garden

*Further Adventures with
the Purple Crayon*

Harold's
Fairy Tale

*by
Crockett
Johnson*

📖 HarperCollins*Publishers*

One evening Harold got out of bed, took his
purple crayon and the moon along, and went
for a walk in an enchanted garden.

Nothing grew in it. If he hadn't known it
was an enchanted garden, Harold scarcely
would have called it a garden at all.

To find out what the trouble was, Harold
decided to ask the king.

Kings live in large castles. Harold had to
make sure the castle was big enough to be
the king's.

He didn't want to waste time talking to

any princes or earls, or dukes.

This was a king's castle all right. It had

tall towers and a big draw-gate to keep out

people the king didn't want to see.

But when the draw-gate was drawn closed

it kept Harold out too.

Harold shouted for the king to come down
and let him in. But the gate didn't open.

He walked along the edge of the enchanted

garden beside the smooth wall of the castle

—until he thought of his purple crayon.

A person smaller than a very small mouse
would be able to get in.

Without even bending, he walked into a
very small mousehole.

He walked through the mousehole into
the castle. He invited the mouse in too,
but the mouse preferred to stay outside.

As he gazed around inside the big castle
Harold felt very tiny.

And a king might not pay much attention

to anybody who was smaller than a mouse.

So Harold used his purple crayon again.

He made sure he was as tall as four and
a half steps of stairs, his usual height.

Then he climbed up the stairs, looking

for the king.

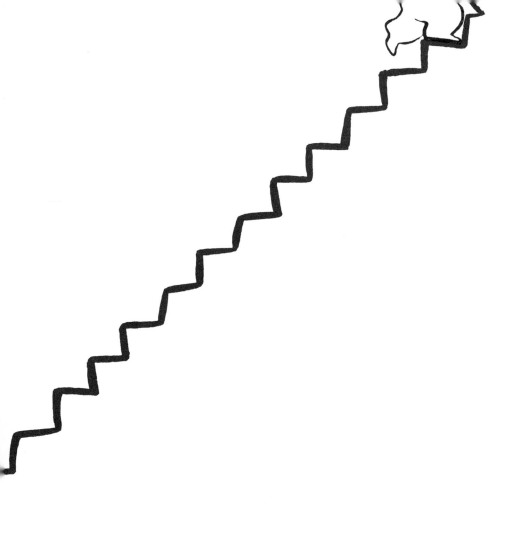

He went up and up and up, until he got so
tired he couldn't climb another step.

Luckily there were no more steps. He had
reached the top.

He still couldn't find the king. But he
remembered kings sat on thrones.

The king's throne looked very comfortable.
Harold thought the king wouldn't mind if
he rested a few minutes.

He sat on the throne, wondering what it

was like to be a king and wear a crown.

He tried it, with the king's crown.

It was all right for a while. But the
crown began to feel heavy.

So Harold put it on the king's head.

As he thanked the king for the loan of
the crown, he noticed the king looked
sad—no doubt because of the garden.

He asked the king if the trouble was due
to a witch or a giant. The king couldn't
say which. He looked sad and helpless.

Evidently the giant or witch—if the king

couldn't tell which it was—was invisible.

But Harold told the king not to worry.

He set off to find the invisible witch or giant, brandishing his purple crayon. And —accidently—it made a hole in the wall.

The accident embarrassed Harold. But
the hole was the handiest way out of the
castle and he climbed through it.

When he looked down from the other side
of the hole, he realized he had forgotten
how high up he was.

He needed something tall to climb down

on, something as tall as a steeple.

To fill the hole in the castle, Harold put

a handsome and useful clock in it. He was

surprised to see how late it was.

He slid down the steeple, to find the
invisible witch or giant right away.

It wasn't a steeple. It was a pointed hat.

It was a GIANT WITCH.

The purple crayon made it plain—it was
an invisible giant witch. Well, no wonder
nothing grew in the enchanted garden.

How could anything grow, Harold said
to himself, with a giant witch tramping
around with big feet.

Now that he saw what the trouble was, all
Harold had to do was drive the witch out
of the enchanted garden.

Mosquitoes. Mosquitoes, Harold knew, will

drive anybody out of a garden.

The mosquitoes drove out the witch. They also were driving Harold out of the garden.

He had to make smoke to get rid of the
mosquitoes.

And he had once heard somebody say that
where there's smoke there must be fire.

To put out the fire, he first thought of
fire engines. But he decided to make it
rain. Rain was easier.

The rain soaked everything—Harold too.

But, he said, it's good for the flowers.

He was right. Soon there were flowers.

Beautiful flowers popped up all over the enchanted garden, more than Harold was able to count, all in gorgeous bloom.

Harold thought how delighted and happy
the king would be when he looked out
from the castle in the morning.

And then, amazingly, the last flower
turned out to be not a flower at all—
but a lovely fairy.

She held out her magic wand as fairies

always do when they're giving somebody

wishes that will come true.

Harold couldn't think of a thing to wish
for. But, to be polite, he took one wish
and told the fairy he'd use it later.

Besides, Harold thought, as he started on his long walk home, a wish might come in handy sometime.

After all the excitement he suddenly felt
tired. And he stopped to rest awhile.

He sat on a small rug because the ground
was still somewhat damp from the rain.
And he wished—

He wished the rug was a flying carpet.

At once Harold felt it rise in the air.

It flew fast and high.

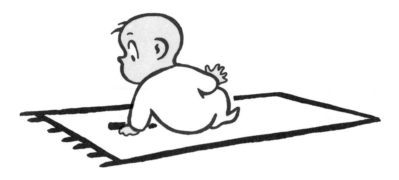

But when it went so fast it left the moon

behind, Harold realized he didn't know how

to stop the carpet, or even slow it down.

He wished he'd taken two wishes from the
fairy, so he could wish the flying carpet
would land.

But he did have his purple crayon.

He landed the flying carpet in his living
room, right behind the high-backed chair
his mother sat in, knitting.

And he asked her to read him a story
before he went back to bed.

More Adventures with the Purple Crayon

Harold's Trip to the Sky

by Crockett Johnson

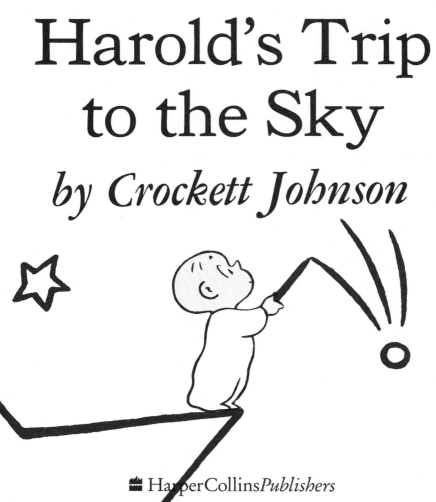

HarperCollins*Publishers*

Copyright © 1957 by Crockett Johnson
Copyright renewed 1985 by Ruth Krauss
All rights reserved. Printed in the U.S.A.
Library of Congress catalog card number: 57–9262
ISBN: 0–06–443025–1 (pbk.)

One night Harold got up, made sure there
was a moon so he wouldn't see things in the
dark, and went to get a drink of water.

He wondered about the things people see in the dark, and where they came from. He was glad he couldn't see them in the moonlight.

Suddenly he realized he didn't see anything
at all in the moonlight. There was nothing
to see. He was in the middle of a desert.

No wonder he was so thirsty. But, luckily,
he had brought his purple crayon.

And he knew where to find water on a desert.

There was always a pool of it somewhere near a palm tree.

Harold drank deeply. There is nothing like
drinking nice cool water on a desert.

But there isn't much else to do on a desert,
Harold realized as he looked around, except
maybe play in the sand.

Then he remembered how the government
has fun on the desert. It shoots off rockets.

Harold decided to go to the moon.

On a good fast rocket, he figured, he could
get there and back in time for breakfast.

He fired the rocket.

And off he went.

But the rocket missed the moon. It missed
it by a mile. And Harold went up and up.

Up and up, he went, into the dark.

Harold tried to see where he was going by
the stars. He tried planets and comets.

What he really needed to light his way was
another moon.

But when Harold looked closely, what he
saw wasn't a moon. To his amazement,
it was a flying saucer.

Harold had heard about flying saucers.
People saw them in the dark. And nobody
knew who was inside, flying them.

He decided he had better land his rocket
right away.

He landed it, with a bump, on the bottom
of a strange planet.

There was no danger of falling off so big
a planet.

However, Harold thought he would feel a little more comfortable at the top.

He wondered what planet he was on.

In the dark light of the stars he looked for
some sign that might tell him.

He was on Mars.

Harold had heard of men on Mars. So he
yelled a couple of hellos, hopefully.

He thought of the flying saucer out there.
He thought of the things people see in the
dark. He felt a great need for company.

He was sure any man on Mars would be cordial to a visitor like Harold who had come all this way to chat with him.

He had to draw on his scanty knowledge of
what a man on Mars looked like.

But his looks wouldn't matter in the dark,
so Harold didn't care much what he turned
out to look like.

All Harold wanted was to know there was
some sort of friendly face close by, even if
he couldn't see it clearly in the dark.

Then, all of a sudden, Harold did see it
clearly. It was the face of a thing.

It was a thing people see in the dark.
And it was sitting in a flying saucer.

Harold ran.

Then he thought and stopped. Probably
the thing was about to fly to earth and
scare somebody, maybe some little child.

Bravely Harold crept back.

He approached on tiptoe, so the thing
wouldn't hear him. And he reached out
with his purple crayon.

And he put a completely damaging crack
in the flying saucer.

Before the thing could grab him he was
off again, chuckling triumphantly.

He ran as fast as he could in the dark.

Happily, most of the way was down hill.

He hoped he wouldn't fall head over heels.

He arrived safely, heels over head, at the bottom of Mars where the rocket was.

But by this time Harold had had enough
of adventure. He wanted to get home in
a dependable way.

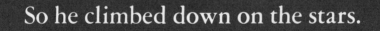

So he climbed down on the stars.

It was sure but slow. And the points of
the stars hurt his feet. Harold wished he
were home.

He recalled that the best way to wish is
on a good big shooting star.

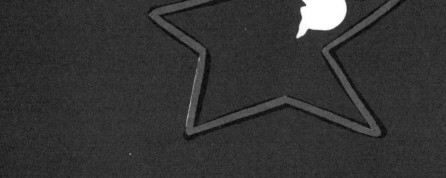

Instead of wishing, it occurred to him at
the last moment to jump aboard.

He shot right down to earth, where he made
a neat two-point landing.

He hadn't passed the moon on the way and he wondered what had happened to it. It wasn't anywhere around.

Then he realized the night was just about
gone and it was time for the sun to come up.
He was hungry.

The sun appeared right on time.

It came up big and bright. Harold remarked
that it was going to be a nice day.

Nobody was ever bothered by flying saucers
and things in the sunshine.

But, for a startled moment, he thought he saw a flying saucer. It was on the horizon, looking as if it had just come in to land.

He was mistaken. It wasn't a saucer. It
was an oatmeal bowl.

Harold happened to like hot breakfasts.

He quickly drew up a chair.

And he sat down to eat.

HAROLD'S
CIRCUS

An Astounding Colossal, Purple Crayon Event!

HAROLD'S CIRCUS

by Crockett Johnson

🏭 HarperCollins*Publishers*

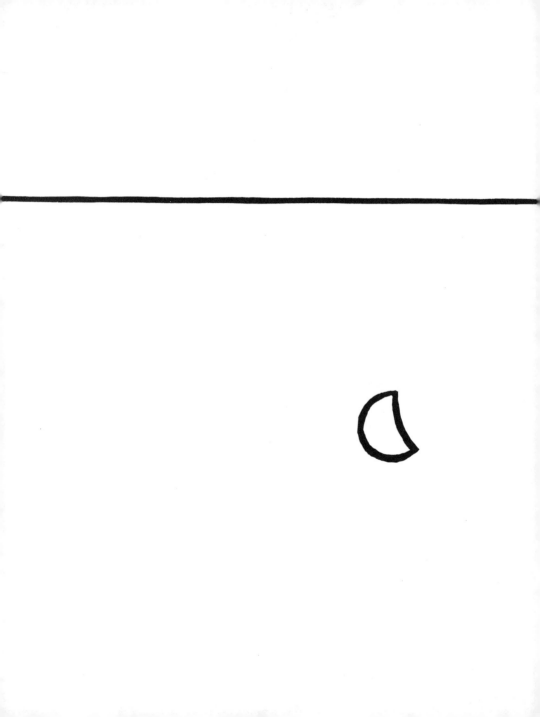

One moonlit evening, mainly to prove to himself he could do it, Harold went for a walk on a tightrope.

He made sure the rope was drawn tight
and straight, so it wouldn't sway.

He skipped lightly across it, finding it fun to be a tightrope walker, high up over the rest of the circus.

He stayed up on the rope with the greatest of ease, until he lost his balance.

It also is easy to fall off a tightrope.

Harold fell, twisting and turning, with
his purple crayon tight in his hand.

By a stroke of luck, a comfortable-looking curve appeared beneath him.

And he landed on an elephant's trunk.

Quite a trick, he thought, as he rewarded
the elephant with a large peanut.

Elephants are such tall animals. Harold
was still a long way from the ground.

So he swung down from the elephant's trunk to the neck of a smaller animal.

It was a lovely circus horse, beautifully
trained, and Harold easily put him into
a brisk trot.

Harold rode with no saddle, in a splendid
exhibition of circus riding.

At the finish of his bareback act he leapt
gracefully from the horse.

To his embarrassment, he fell and turned a rather ridiculous somersault.

Before anyone could laugh at the mishap
Harold pretended he had been clowning.

He quickly put on a clown's hat.

He put a clown's smile on his face. And
he acted silly, like a clown.

Finally he took off the hat and the smile.

And he gave them back to the clown.

The real clown was extremely funny. And
Harold laughed and laughed at him.

This, Harold told himself, probably was
the best circus he had ever seen in his life.

Like all circuses, it had a fat lady.

She was really amazingly fat.

And, of course, there was a very tall man.

He was really astoundingly tall.

And next to him was a very small man.

There was another man, a lemonade man.

He had a great tank of lemonade.

Harold stopped for a drink of it, through a straw. It was quite refreshing.

He left some money on the counter to pay
for the drink and he went on, looking for
the man who is shot out of a cannon.

Harold wasn't sure what a man who is shot
out of a cannon would look like.

But, anyway, he wasn't there, though the
cannon was nearly ready.

A circus can't wait. There was only one
thing to do.

The cannon fitted Harold perfectly.

He got into it.

And he shot out of it.

He went up fast.

He sailed to the top of the circus, where
the trapezes are, and the flying rings.

He reached out.

He caught on to a flying ring.

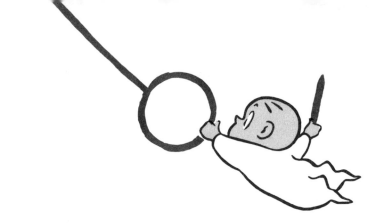

He swung far out on it.

He let go, doing a startling flip-flop in the air, and he dived straight down.

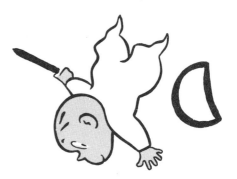

He was sure the elephant would be there
to catch him again.

Once more, a reassuring curve appeared
beneath him.

But he landed surprisingly hard. This was no elephant's trunk.

It was the tail of a lion. Somehow a lion
had gotten loose in the circus.

Before anyone could quite recognize the
danger and become alarmed, Harold was
at work getting the lion into a cage.

He got into the cage himself, with nothing
but a lion tamer's chair.

Then, like the bravest of lion tamers, he faced the lion.

With no thought of fear, he put his head
right in the lion's mouth.

After he took his head out of the lion's
mouth it occurred to him that lions have
big teeth.

And, suddenly, he became a bit frightened
at how brave he had been.

But his own feelings didn't matter, Harold
told himself as he left the lion's cage.

The important thing at a circus is to make
the audience happy.

Harold saw that everybody in his audience
wore a delighted smile.

Naturally, making so many people happy
made Harold happy.

And he smiled too as, very modestly,
he bowed.